Gabriel Kelley: Chicago Detective

Alydia Rackham

Published by Alydia Rackham, 2024.

CHAPTER ONE: Silver Lining

CHICAGO, 1931

HE DIDN'T KNOW HOW he was going to get home. To complicate matters, he was alone, and without his badge.

And his right knee wasn't in great shape.

Detective Gabriel Kelley cleared his throat and stepped out of the alley, raking a hand through his mussed hair and straightening his tie as he did. He fought against limping, but couldn't quite succeed. He glanced up at the dim streetlight that cast a dirty halo upon the sidewalk and street. Traffic wasn't too heavy at this time of night, unfortunately. He wouldn't be able to grab a cab now, even if he had his wallet.

Which he didn't.

Grimacing, he started up the sidewalk, heading for the nearest corner. He needed to get his bearings. He passed the darkened windows and barred doors, glancing at the signs, hoping to catch sight of something familiar. He had limped two blocks, though, before he did. He saw a flickering neon sign above a shuttered door that read Paulie's Donuts.

"Wait a second," he muttered. "Isn't this...?"

The next moment, he heard it. The crisp, metallic clicking of copper shoe studs against paving...

And the skillful whistling of the tune Molly Malone.

Then, around the bend strolled a cop. He twirled a billy club as he walked, a little sprightly hitch in his step. He was a short man with a dark mustache, an impeccable uniform, with his hat cocked at an angle. Gabriel would know him anywhere.

"McGann?" he called in surprise.

The policeman instantly halted, peering straight at Gabriel...

"Gabe Kelley, my lad!" he suddenly cried in a pleasing Irish lilt, breaking into a smile. "What are ya doin' on my beat, now? Got yerself into a bit o' trouble?"

The next moment, Mick McGann had closed the distance and vigorously shaken Gabriel's hand.

"Yeah, I had a bit of trouble," Gabriel confessed.

"Ah, chasin' after Harry the Mask again, eh?" Mick gave him a shrewd look and put his fists on his hips. "What's that old rascal up to now?"

"Murder," Gabriel sighed, running his hand through his hair again.

"Murder!" Mick repeated, eyebrows raised. "And who would the unlucky fella be, then?"

"Can't tell you that, Mick, I'm sorry," Gabriel smiled wanly. "Wish I could."

"Ah, that's all right, quite all right," Mick waved it off. "I understand. Can't be talkin' out o' turn now, can we? If we learned one thing in the war, that was it."

"Yes, it was," Gabriel agreed grimly. "But at least I can tell you that I was following a lead, got a bit in over my head and lost my jacket and my hat."

"Oh, no, not yer hat," Mick said regretfully. "That was a handsome hat it was, I remember it well."

"Yeah, it was my favorite."

"And ye say ye lost yer jacket too, then?" Mick peered at him. "Ain't ye got any money, then?" "Not a cent," Gabriel admitted. Mick looked him up and down.

"Looks like yer not walkin' too straight either, if ye don't mind me sayin' so," he noted. "Had to jump out a window," Gabriel grunted, bending down to feel the tender joint of his knee. Mick clicked his tongue.

"Sorry to hear that, so sorry," he said. "I'd give you a buck, so I would, if I had any on me—but we're not allowed to carry any valuables at all while we're on the beat."

"I know that, Mick, and I wouldn't ask you anyway," Gabriel smiled at him. Mick watched him in concern for a moment, then reached out and put a hand on his arm.

"I tell you what, though," he proposed. "Just up the street here and to the right one block is a little pub called O'Brian's. Now, it ain't allowed to sell a pint o' Guinness anymore—which, between you and me, is quite a shame—but the manager's a cousin of mine, and the place is open all night. Name's Michael O'Tanner, and if you mention that you're a friend of mine and I sent you, he'll help you out."

"I couldn't do that, Mick—"

"You'll do it, and there'll be no arguin'," Mick said severely, holding up a finger. "Go on, now,

and I'll not hear of you loiterin' about on my streets at this time o' night. Understand?"

Gabriel saw the twinkle in his friend's eye, and smiled at it.

"Thanks, Mick."

"Good luck, Kelley," Mick slapped his arm. "We'll sit down and have a cuppa tea one of these days."

"Yes, we will," Gabriel agreed. And with that, they parted ways—and Gabriel dutifully headed toward O'Brian's.

The tavern looked just like all the other Irish pubs in Chicago: dark wood interior, walls completely crowded with old photographs and rugby memorabilia, along with Irish sayings and jokes. Lamps burned low, and the corner booths stood in darkness. Gabriel only caught sight of one other patron: a grizzled, toothless old man in a flat cap hunched over a small plate of fish and chips.

A young, red-headed man in a waiter's uniform appeared, and smiled at Gabriel. "Hullo," he greeted him. "Are ye here for breakfast? You'd just make it," he said, glancing down at his watch. "We start serving at four."

"Unfortunately, I don't have any money," Gabriel answered wearily. "Are you Michael

O'Tanner? I was sent here by Mick McGann—I just met him about a block over. He told me you were his cousin, and to tell you I was his friend."

"Mick sent you?" Mr. O'Tanner raised his eyebrows. "Must be in some sorta trouble then, eh?"

"You could say that," Gabriel winced again. "Hurt my knee on the job, lost my wallet and my coat."

Mr. O'Tanner watched him carefully.

"What is it ye do for a livin', then?"

"I'm a detective," Gabriel told him. "But I used to work a beat with Mick a few years ago." Again, Mr. O'Tanner studied him.

"And...so what can I do for ye?"

"I'd just be grateful for a warm place to sit down for a minute," Gabriel sighed. "Get off this bum leg and rest before I have to walk all the way home."

Mr. O'Tanner smiled at him now, and nodded.

"Aye, I think I could do that. Come with me." He beckoned, turned and headed to the far corner of the room to a booth just beneath a lamp, where old photos of Irish bare-knuckle boxers hung.

"Have a seat, rest as long as you'd like," Mr. O'Tanner bid him, and Gabriel gratefully eased down into a seat. Groaning, he rubbed his face, trying to ignore the throbbing in his leg.

He had some idea of where he was in the city, now—but he was a long way away from his apartment, still. The hike would take him several hours...

And by the time he got back, he'd have to change clothes and go right to work.

The idea gave him a headache.

"Here y'are, Mr. Kelley."

Gabriel's head came up—

And Mr. O'Tanner set a hot plate of chips and half of a battered cod fish down in front of him.

Gabriel sat back.

"What—No, I can't pay for this, I've lost my wallet—"

"On the house, sir," Mr. O'Tanner said proudly. "Had a bit o' extra after feedin' old Mr. Piper there." He jerked his head toward the grizzled old man in the other booth. "Least I can do for a fellow

Irishman down on his luck."

Gabriel stared at him. This morning as he'd traipsed to work, Gabriel had observed a bread line that looked to be half a mile long. And here Mr. O'Tanner was actually giving him food...?

"I really can't accept this," he tried.

"Eat up, and stop grousin'," Mr. O'Tanner countered. "I'll not have me fine fish go to waste.

Here, here's some ketchup." And he clomped a bottle of tomato ketchup down on the table.

"Well...thank you, Mr. O'Tanner," Gabriel managed.

"Think nothin' of it," Mr. O'Tanner smiled. "I'm sure ye'd do the same for me."

"You can count on it," Gabriel nodded gravely.

When Mr. O'Tanner left, Gabriel obediently started in on his unexpected meal. The chips were buttery and flavorful, and the fish flakey and delicious. He couldn't remember the last time he'd sat down at a restaurant and eaten a hot meal.

When he'd cleaned his plate, he picked it up as he stood, and found Mr. O'Tanner.

"Thanks for breakfast," he smiled, handing the plate to him. "Ought to keep me full the rest of the day."

"That's th' idea, Mr. Kelley," Mr. O'Tanner beamed. "Come back any time."

"I will. And I'll bring my wallet," Gabriel assured him.

"And a girl?" Mr. O'Tanner said pointedly. Gabriel hesitated a moment, then nodded.

"Yes. And a girl."

"Cheers, then," Mr. O'Tanner waved at him, and Gabriel stepped out into the very early morning—though it was still dark.

Though he had been grateful for the respite, his knee still hurt, and as he walked, he ground his teeth. He watched the occasional car rumble past, and eyed the rare pedestrian, but kept on a straight track down the dirty streets.

Then, at about five in the morning...

It began to rain.

Just a sprinkling at first, then a steady drizzle, then an outright rain. He had no hat to shield his face, and no coat to turn up his collar. He could only fold his arms and duck from awning to awning, his shoes splashing through puddles. The water coursed down the bricks of the buildings and ran over the sidewalks into the gutters. It filled the dingy streets with noise, and muffled the engines of the one or two cars.

However, one or two cars soon became ten or fifteen, then twenty, then hundreds. They rumbled through the downpour, their windshield wipers beating, their tires splashing waves of water up onto the curbs. Also, more people began to appear, venturing out into the streets to head to work, if they were lucky—or to the unemployment office or breadlines if they were not.

But every single one of them had an umbrella.

Black umbrellas crowded the streets, jostling each other as people tried to find the correct lane of foot traffic. Gabriel tried his best not to intrude upon anyone's space—but as the rain pelted him harder and harder, he wished he could duck beneath a tall man's canvas and just trail along behind him.

In a few minutes, as the sky barely lightened with the sunrise, the rain became a torrent. It ran into his eyes and beat on his head and shoulders. He couldn't stand it anymore.

He ducked into the scant cover of a covered bus stop, gasping and swiping the rain out of his face. He halfway noticed that he shared the little area with four other people: three men, and a plaindressed woman in her forties. For a few moments, the traffic splashed by and the rain poured—but he was away from it, at least for a while.

"What's happened to you?"

He glanced over at the woman, who had spoken.

It's true, she was plainly dressed—but she had dark, serious eyes and a pretty face, and she was watching him curiously. He laughed faintly, again wiping at his face.

"I've...Well, I've had a heck of a day so far," he muttered, deciding to go with a fictionalized story rather than the truth, of course. "Cab got in an accident and I had to get out when the cops got there, and I left my hat, jacket and wallet in the cab. I'm hoping they took them to the police station."

"Can't you call your wife and ask her to go look?" the lady asked. Gabriel smiled crookedly.

"Haven't got a wife."

"Well," she stated. "There's your trouble."

Gabriel chuckled.

"Probably so, ma'am."

She watched him for another moment...

Then pulled the loop of her small umbrella off her left wrist.

"Here. Take this for your walk."

"Oh, no, ma'am, I can't," Gabriel said quickly.

"Why not? I have ten umbrellas at home," she said. "My father worked for an umbrella factory—Mother's got an entire closet full." She pushed it at him. "Take it, or I will hit you with it." Gabriel did laugh now, and took it from her.

"Thank you, ma'am."

"You're quite welcome," she said, smiling at him now. "I hope you have good luck retrieving your things."

Soon, the bus arrived, and the women and the three men boarded it. Gabriel watched her go... Then opened the new umbrella and stepped out again into the torrent.

He walked for another two hours, though not very quickly. His right shoe had begun to pain him now, and he knew he would have a wicked blister soon. He could not complain, though. The lady's umbrella felt like a godsend.

At about seven in the morning, the rain finally ceased—but now a brisk wind blew, and, since he was wet to the bone, it cut through him like a knife. He knew exactly where he was, now...

But he didn't think he could walk any more. Not without risking putting himself in the hospital.

Shivering, he took refuge under a bright red canopy and leaned back against the cold brick wall. He would just have to wait until a cop car drove by, and flag it down. That's what he would have to do.

The door to his left swung open violently and the bell jangled. Gabriel whirled around— A black-haired teenager wearing the usual clothes of a diner busboy burst out and jerked his head, giving Gabriel a stern look.

"Tony says get in here," he barked.

"What?" Gabriel said in surprise. The boy waved his arm in a huge gesture of beckoning and gave him an impatient look.

"Tony says get in here," he ordered.

"Tony...?" Gabriel blinked, frowning, and trailed into the business...

Suddenly realizing where he was.

A long, narrow diner, with booths to the left and a bar with stools to the right, flooded with customers, noise, and the intoxicating scent of frying bacon. The busboy ushered Gabriel down the bar toward a thickset, young Italian man behind the counter taking orders on a notepad. But when he saw Gabriel, he stuffed the notepad into his apron and gave him a huge smile.

"Well, well, well, if it ain't Gabe Kelley," he declared, sticking out his hand. "You look like something the cat dragged in. What gives?"

"How are you, Morelli?" Gabriel asked, shaking his hand.

"Business is good, it's good," Tony Morelli nodded emphatically. "How's yours?"

"Not so good," Gabriel grunted. "Being out on the job last night cost me my coat, my hat and my wallet."

"Where was you?" Morelli asked, frowning.

"East side," Gabriel rubbed his face. Morelli raised his eyebrows.

"All the way out there? And whadja do, walk here?"

"Yeah," Gabriel sighed. Morelli swore.

"I ain't havin' this," he declared. "The 'tec who saved my old man's life ain't gonna be hoofing it all the way down to the station, not on my watch. You sit right here, my friend, I'll be with you in just a sec."

"Tony—" Gabriel tried, but Morelli had already charged back into the kitchen.

"Hey, siddown," the busboy snapped, and pointed at the empty stool. Chagrined, Gabriel did so. The next second, as if by magic, a hot cup of coffee appeared in front of him—brought by a pretty but very quick waitress. As he sipped, and the hot drink warmed him down to his bones, he listened to the raucous conversation of all the patrons filling the place like thunder.

A few minutes later, when he had all but drained the cup, Gabriel spotted Morelli returning.

The next second, Morelli lifted Gabriel's hand and slapped money into it.

"Cab fare," Morelli said. "Now get yourself home."

"Tony, no," Gabriel insisted, trying to give it back. "I can walk—"

"I ain't takin' it back," Morelli backed away and threw his hands in the air. "Either take it or give it to the panhandler on the corner, but I ain't takin' it."

Slowly, Gabriel lowered his hand, and smiled at him.

"Thanks, Tony."

"You bet, Kelley," Morelli smiled, and nodded. "Anything else I can do, you just let me know." "Likewise," Gabriel told him earnestly. "Thanks for the coffee."

"No problem!"

Feeling a great deal warmer, Gabriel shook Morelli's hand again, and ventured out onto the street, his new umbrella still on his arm. It only took him a minute to hail a cab, and to gratefully climb inside.

And as he shut the door, and gave the driver the address of his apartment, he gazed out at the cloudy, busy, rushing city.

Perhaps he'd been wrong.

Perhaps he wasn't so alone after all.

And perhaps this whole city—even with all its messes and corruptions, crime and danger... Was actually home.

CHAPTER TWO: Three Words

CHICAGO, 1931

"I love you," Penny said into the receiver. Nothing but phonograph music and some sort of rustling replied. She frowned. "Did you hear me, Mother? I love you."

"Oh, yes! Yes, dear, I heard you," came her mother's slightly frazzled voice at the other end. "I love you, too."

"Well, give a kiss to Dad for me," Penny smiled. "Looking forward to seeing you on Sunday." "We'll be having fried chicken and dumplings, and apple pie," her mother said. "Oh, I forgot to send Dad to the Masons' to get the apples. Henry? Henry, I need you to go down to the Masons to get those apples. What? No, it can't wait till tomorrow, I need to start peeling them tonight. Yes, I do!"

"All right, I'll talk to you later, Mom," Penny laughed.

"Oh—yes, dear. And you be careful on that train. I've read so many awful stories in the newspaper lately. Are you sure you don't want Dad to come in the truck to get you?"

"No, the traffic here is too difficult," Penny assured her. "Really, on Sundays the train isn't busy at all. Don't worry about me."

"I always worry about you, working for that detective," her mother answered, and Penny could feel her frown. "A lady like you, keeping company with all kinds of criminals and loose women..."

"Not at all, Mother," Penny assured her. "I sit here all day and type, that's all."

"Good," her mother declared. "And I hope it stays that way."

Of course, Penny had decided long ago not to mention her various run-ins with Harry the Mask and other such gangsters during her work with Detective Kelley. She couldn't bear to worry her mother...

"I'm sure it will," Penny smiled. "Talk to you later."

"I love you dear. See you soon. Goodbye!"

"I love you! Goodbye!" Penny replied, and hung up the phone. She took a deep breath as she glanced around the little office space. The walls were painted beige, the mop boards and frames around the doors a dark wood. To her right, a small window let in the very early morning light. Straight in front of her, smiling placidly, hung a small, slightly crooked portrait of John Adams. Mr. Kelley had hung it there upon moving in, citing John Adams' excellent record as a lawyer and pillar of unbiased justice before he ever began a career in politics and nation-building. Penny smiled back at the old founding father.

To her left stood the closed door to the inner office, its smoked glass marked with the painted words DETECTIVE GABRIEL KELLEY. Mr. Kelley had not come in yet—he had been out on a case late into last night, and Penny doubted he would come in before ten. She sighed and adjusted the stack of papers on her immaculately organized desk. She might as well take care of one thing while it was still quiet.

She drew out a piece of stationery and her pen, then put on her reading glasses and began to write.

Brother of mine,

How are you, Steve? Will you be able to make it home next month for Dad's birthday? I know he is counting on you to go fishing with him. Perhaps you could ask your foreman for half a day off, so that you could arrive a bit early and surprise him. Mom would be thrilled too. I, on the other hand, will simply tolerate you. Hahaha...

More news here that you don't dare mention to the folks:

We've had three interesting cases this past month: one involved a very glamorous blonde divorcee who swore that her ex-husband had stolen her wedding ring, when in fact it had been stolen by her secret lover! Ah, her face when Mr. Kelley brought him into the room in front of her husband...

Another was a hooch distillery being run right underneath a drugstore. A huge operation! And it was uncovered by a woman who worked at the drugstore who kept telling her employer that she smelled something "funny," and he kept telling her she ought to see a doctor! Hahaha...

Another was a murder, I am sorry to say, and the case is unfortunately ongoing. I can't tell you much, as a great deal of it is under wraps, but as usual, we suspect Harry the Mask and his men. You'll read about it in the papers, no doubt, along with a great many grisly details that have been completely fabricated by those ridiculous newspapermen. I warn you, don't believe a word they say!

As always, Mr. Kelley is devoted to his work, almost to distraction. I often have to send out for a sandwich to make certain he's eaten something throughout the day, and if I don't remind him, sometimes he does not shave, or put on a different tie. It is too bad, too, because he is a very handsome man when he cleans and polishes himself up a little. But these gangsters have him so infuriated, and he is so determined to catch them and put them behind bars, I wonder if he thinks of anything else—even sleeping.

Anyway, I hope work is going well for you. I say again how thankful I am that you've kept your job, and I've kept mine, and that we can send extra money home to Mom and Dad. The bread lines here are stretching around the block sometimes...

Write me back soon, little brother, whenever you have the time.

I love you,

Sis

SHE FOLDED THE LETTER, put it in the envelope and addressed it by memory, and put a stamp on it, then set it in the outgoing basket on her desk. Then, clearing her throat and sitting up, she took a fresh piece of paper, rolled it noisily into her faithful typewriter, then fished out the first file folder. This morning, she would be typing up the notes she had taken in shorthand whilst listening to Mr. Kelley interview suspects and other people of interest in this murder case.

Her quick eyes flew over her shorthand notes and the typewriter clattered like the well-oiled machine it was. When she paused to re-read, she could hear the dull rumble of the many other typewriters throughout the building clattering just as hers did. All the other lady secretaries to the policemen, detectives and other officers, hard at work at 8 a.m.

She answered various phone calls as she worked, took messages and stacked them neatly by her left hand, and made her way through six pages of notes before standing up, stretching, and leaving the office for a few minutes to snatch a cup of coffee from the common room. Then, she resumed her typing, the rich scent of her beverage filling the little room.

At half past nine, she heard footsteps on the lower stairs. She paused, listening—

And in an instant confirmed who it was.

She pulled off her reading glasses—she never liked for him to see her wearing them—and got to her feet, picking up the stack of messages.

In a moment, the front door of the office opened, and Detective Gabriel Kelley strode in. He wore a dark suit and tie, the white collar of his shirt slightly crooked. When he took off his fedora and hung it on the hat stand, Penny saw that he had combed back his dark hair, and shaved his angular, good-looking face. His solemn brow was absently furrowed, as usual, and his brilliant black eyes found her for a moment as he crossed toward his door.

"Good morning, Mr. Kelley," she greeted him, smiling brightly.

"Morning, Penny," he sighed, digging in his pocket for his office key.

"We've gotten six messages this morning—individual ones, I should say. The commissioner called twice," Penny said, handing him the pile of written messages.

"Doesn't give an inch, does he?" Mr. Kelley muttered, shuffling through the messages before returning to his key and opening the door.

He stepped through and left the door open, heading to his desk. Penny followed him.

"Sleep all right?" she asked, watching him.

"All right, I guess," he said, rounding the messy desk and sitting down in the squeaky chair, setting the messages down beside the telephone. But as Penny studied him, she wondered if he had gone to bed at all. He was wearing the same tie as yesterday. He may have only put on a new jacket. She tried not to wince.

"Have any breakfast?"

"I had an egg at the hotel." He rubbed his eyes. "Get me a cup of coffee, will you, Pen? And get me..." he snapped his fingers as he screwed his eyes shut. "...get me—"

"Lionel on the phone?" she supplied. He opened his eyes and pointed at her—and gave her a slight smile.

"Lionel on the phone."

She smiled back at him.

"Of course, Mr. Kelley."

Penny left the room and fetched the coffee, making it just the way he liked it: black, with one cube of sugar. When she returned and set it on his desk, he was busily writing.

"Thanks, Pen," he murmured, frowning as he wrote.

"Of course," she said quietly. "I'll get Lionel."

She hurried out and sat down, then called up Lionel Stage, the chief of police, and forwarded the call to Mr. Kelley's office. When his phone rang in there, he got up and shut the door, and conducted a lengthy conversation in private. Penny continued to translate her shorthand notes on the typewriter.

At noon, she put all of her work inside a locked drawer, picked up the outgoing mail, and knocked on Mr. Kelley's door.

"Yeah?" he called. She opened the door to see him sitting back in his chair, turned toward her right, gazing distantly up at the calendar—the only thing that hung on that wall.

"I'm going to lunch," Penny said. "Salami on rye?"

"And a Coca-Cola," he added quietly. "Thanks, Pen."

"Of course," she said, and slipped out. She retrieved her hat, jacket and purse, then hurried down the hall, down the elevator, and into the lobby of the office building. She dropped off the mail, then stepped out onto the busy Chicago streets. The air filled with the noise and smoke of traffic, and people of all sorts bustled past her as she hurried down the sidewalk.

She didn't live far away, thankfully, and it did not take her long to reach her apartment building. When she entered, she greeted her landlady, Mrs. Rollings, whom she paid a little extra to make her lunch and dinner.

"I'll be down in a minute, Mrs. Rollings, I just need to say hello to Charlie," Penny said to the smiling lady, before dashing up two flights of stairs to her little apartment.

When she opened the door, her little black and white cat greeted her with meows and purring, and affectionate rubbing against her legs. She picked him up and cuddled him, admiring, as always, the neat little black spot on his white face, just beneath his nose. It made him look just like Charlie Chaplin. Hence the name.

Penny spent several minutes cuddling and scratching the cat, refilling his food bowl, making certain he had enough water, and playing with him with a piece of string. At last, she excused herself to go eat lunch.

"See you later, Charlie. I love you," she said, kissing him on the head as he purred even louder.

She secured her door and went back downstairs to sit in Mrs. Rollings' comfortable, homey yellow kitchen, eating homemade chicken noodle soup and listening to the news about the other tenants from Mrs. Rollings. Penny loved to listen to the good woman's amusing conversation while the landlady washed dishes and dried them. It reminded Penny so much of her own mother in the kitchen.

About half an hour later, Penny arose, did her own dishes, and said goodbye to Mrs. Rollings.

"Thank you for lunch, Mrs. Rollings," she said—as always. "I love you!"

"I love you too, dear girl!" Mrs. Rollings answered, and she meant it.

After reapplying her lipstick and popping a mint into her mouth, Penny hurried out to the street again. Almost back to the office, she stopped in at Mr. Kelley's favorite deli and ordered him the exact sandwich he liked, and a Coca-Cola—along with a slice of chocolate pie as a surprise. She carried the bag into the building with her and up the elevator, then hurried into their office.

She replaced her coat, hat and purse, then took her boss' lunch in to him. He was on the phone when she entered, in a heated discussion with Lionel, it sounded like, so she just left it on the desk and sat back down to work.

At about two o'clock, Mr. Kelley emerged from his office. Penny quickly looked up from her work and pulled the glasses off her nose.

"You got me a piece of chocolate pie too?" Mr. Kelley asked her.

Penny raised her eyebrows at him, and smiled a little.

"I know you like it, and it was on special today."

Mr. Kelley, tired as he looked, suddenly gave her a genuine smile.

"Thanks, Penny."

"Of course," she grinned back. And he returned to his office.

The rest of the afternoon, she fielded calls and continued typing, and also had to corral a fierce red-headed woman wearing a fox stole who almost barged right into Mr. Kelley's office. It took all of Penny's considerable command to keep her at bay and force her to sit for a few minutes in the waiting chair. When this woman finally had her interview with Mr. Kelley, and then left a short time later in a huff because he had insisted that he was a police detective—not a private eye at leisure to follow her philandering husband around—Penny had rarely felt so relieved to see someone go.

At last, five o'clock rolled around, and Penny finished off her work. She stacked everything inside her locked drawer and turned the key, and then put the key in the little safe in the wall. After gathering her things, she moved to Mr. Kelley's half open door and rapped on it with her knuckles. Mr. Kelley looked up from one of his notebooks filled with crime-scene notations. A strand of his dark hair fell down across his forehead, making him look younger than his thirty-three years. "I'm on my way home, Mr. Kelley," she smiled softly. "Have a good evening."

"Oh. Yeah, goodnight, Penny," he nodded at her. She started to go.

"Thanks for the chocolate pie, Pen," he added. "That was a real treat."

She paused, gazing back at him for a moment and meeting his eyes.

"Of course," she said, her chest tightening. "I..."

She stopped herself. He waited, his brow furrowing a bit.

She swallowed, then smiled and lifted her chin.

"Of course." She backed out of the room and shut the door, heading once more for the outer corridor and the elevator. Feeling her cheeks turn warm.

Two words. Always the same two words to him.

How she wished it could be three.

CHAPTER THREE: The Kid

FINDING HERSELF CAUGHT between two men who were at odds with each other was a bit complex, but when one was thirty-three and the other was eight years old, Penny Creek decided it could be downright amusing.

"Listen, kid," Penny's frazzled boss, Detective Gabriel Kelley, pushed his fedora back on his head and bent forward, bracing his hands on his knees. His dark eyes flashed. "We've been over it a dozen times already—you can't live at the police station."

The eight-year-old boy, sitting on the edge of Mr. Kelley's desk and tossing a baseball back and forth, stopped suddenly and looked up, frowning at the detective. He wore overalls, but no shirt, battered shoes, and a dirty cap. Beneath that cap, Penny could see a shock of blond hair. The boy had large, intelligent blue eyes, and a smattering of freckles across his nose.

"I can so," the boy protested.

"No, you can't," Mr. Kelley argued.

"Oh, yeah? Who says?" the boy shot back.

"I says," Mr. Kelley answered, straightening up again. "Now tell me your name, kiddo." The boy stuck out his lip and shook his head.

"Nope," he said. "Not till you say I can stay here."

"I'm not gonna say that, kid, so you can forget about it." Mr. Kelley rounded the desk and sat down, pulling out a huge phone book from one of the drawers. "Now, what's your dad's name?"

"Nope," the boy replied, tossing the ball higher. "I ain't telling."

"Listen, if you keep being obstinate, I'll just hand you over to the chief, and he'll put you in jail," Mr. Kelley threatened. "What do you think of that?"

The boy turned around on the desk and stared at him, then narrowed his eyes.

"Nuh-uh. They don't put kids in jail."

"You don't think so?" Mr. Kelley raised his eyebrows. "You haven't been around the block enough times."

The boy wrinkled his nose in disbelief, absently tossing the baseball from hand to hand in his lap. Mr. Kelley opened the front cover of the phone book, put his finger down and took a deep breath.

"Aaron, Albert and Sheila. Aaron, Bart and Jenny. Aaron, Bernard and Katherine. Aaron, Castor and Elizabeth."

The boy started to giggle.

"Are you gonna just read the phone book?"

"Yep," Mr. Kelley answered. "And I'm going to call every single one of these people. One of 'em is bound to be your folks."

Penny's eyes widened. She knew it was just a ploy, but based on the smirk on the boy's face, she wagered it had little chance of working.

"What if we go and get you an ice cream?" Penny suddenly spoke up from the corner of the room.

The boy's head whipped around. He stared at her for a moment, then gave her a suspicious
look.

"In exchange for what?"

"Telling us your name," Penny said. He shook his head.

"Nope."

"How about just your first name, then?" she offered.

He hesitated. She smiled at him.

"How about it? Ice cream for your first name?"

He studied her carefully, then lifted her chin.

"Okay. I'll tell you after I have some."

"Sounds like a deal," Penny stepped up to him and held out her hand. The little boy smiled and shook it, then hopped off the desk, heading for the door. Mr. Kelley stood up from the desk.

"Don't tell me you're taking a shine to this stray," he muttered.

Penny glanced at him, finding him already watching her.

"He looks just like the Kid in that Chaplin movie, doesn't he?" she whispered. Mr. Kelley rolled his eyes.

"You and Charlie Chaplin," he muttered. "I swear, you'd probably marry him if he asked."

"I probably would," she answered cheekily. "Shall we go?"

Together, they followed the boy out of the main office and into the area where Penny worked. Mr. Kelley helped Penny into her jacket while the boy watched, and Penny put on her hat and grabbed her purse. In a few moments, they were headed out the door toward the elevator. As the doors opened, the boy began to grin.

"You like elevators?" Penny observed.

"Yes, ma'am," the boy shot a twinkling look up at her.

"I have an idea," she said. "Why don't we take the elevator all the way to the top, and you can take a look at the view from up there before we go down. Want to?"

Mr. Kelley groaned and stuck his hands in his pockets, but Penny ignored him. The boy lit up.

"Sure!"

So Penny asked the attendant to send them straight up, which took them up fifty floors to the top of the building. There, they stepped out into a lounge area with broad windows, through which they could see a great deal of Chicago's downtown skyline. The boy put both hands on the glass, staring wide-eyed. Penny glanced over at Mr. Kelley...

Who was watching the boy. But when he noticed that she had seen him, he looked away.

Penny smiled.

After the boy had thoroughly absorbed the view, they headed back down the elevator—and Penny let him tell the operator which floor. They stepped out into the busy lobby, then out into the street.

They would have to walk about two blocks before coming to an ice cream shop, and since it was about noon, the traffic on the sidewalk bustled noisily. The three stopped just outside the door. "Here, can you hold my hand, please?" Penny asked, reaching down. "I don't want you to get run over or lost."

The boy stared up at her in disbelief, then slowly took her hand. Penny gripped it gently but firmly, then looked over at Mr. Kelley.

"All right, come with me. Stick close," he advised—and took his position on the side of the walk nearest the street. He held out his left arm, and Penny took it. Together, the three of them started along.

They couldn't talk much, due to the traffic noise, so Penny could occasionally glance down and observe the little boy as he gazed seriously all around him, half-frightened, half-amazed.

Soon, they reached the busy ice-cream parlor, and Mr. Kelley opened the door for them. Penny led the boy inside.

The place looked a little shabby, but still retained most of its old ragtime charm: black-andwhite tiled floors, lacy bric-a-brac, mirrors on the walls, and an old soda fountain. Children crowded tables, as it was summertime—but all of them looked better dressed than the little boy whose hand Penny held. A few of them peered over at him curiously, and he frowned back at them, stuffing the baseball in his large pocket. Again, Penny sensed Mr. Kelley watching him.

They stepped up to the counter, and the teenaged boy dressed in a paper cap, striped shirt and apron leaned on the tile top and smiled.

"What'll it be?" he asked.

Penny looked down at the boy.

"What flavor do you want?"

The boy's eyes widened.

"What flavor?" he gaped at her. "There's more than just…ice cream flavored?"

"Sure, kid," Mr. Kelley suddenly spoke up. "All kinds. Raspberry, blueberry, chocolate, mint, strawberry, peanut butter…"

The boy looked at Mr. Kelley with an open mouth. Penny turned to her boss.

"Which is your favorite?"

Mr. Kelley looked at her, then at the boy, and put his hands in his pockets.

"Well. I like chocolate."

"How about a chocolate cone?" Penny smiled at the teenager.

"Coming right up," he said. "That'll be three cents."

Penny started to get into her purse, but then Mr. Kelley whipped out his coin bag and fished out three pennies and laid them down.

"What do you say?" Penny whispered to the boy.

The boy blinked, frowned…

"Thanks?" he tried. She squeezed his hand.

In a flash, the teenager handed the boy his cone, brimming with chocolate ice cream, and swept the pennies into the cash register.

"Why don't we sit by the window?" Penny suggested. Together, the three of them crossed the room and settled into a booth, Penny with the boy, and Mr. Kelley across from them. They didn't talk much, though Penny made light remarks about the people passing by outside, just to fill the silence. Once again, she could see Mr. Kelley carefully watching the boy, studying him, no doubt, for clues to his identity…

But all at once, she sensed it was a little more than that.

The boy enjoyed the ice cream thoroughly. Of course, he could not eat it as slowly as he would have liked, because it began to drip, but the task absorbed him completely. Penny doubted he heard a word she said. He ate the cone, too, and then licked his fingers after.

"Here, use a napkin," she advised, handing him one and also wiping his mouth with another. "Now," Mr. Kelley said quietly. "How about a name?"

The boy looked gravely across at him, still wiping his fingers.

"My first name?" he asked.

"Yep. Your first name," Mr. Kelley nodded.

"My name's Jack."

An unexpected smile flickered across Mr. Kelley's face.

"Jack, huh?" he said. "Sounds like a good name. Named for your dad?"

Jack pursed his lips and shook his head, concentrating on his fingers. "Nope. My uncle."

Penny and Mr. Kelley exchanged a glance.

"Your uncle?" Penny said. "Does your uncle...have a job?"

"Mhm," Jack nodded.

"Where?" Mr. Kelley wondered. Jack looked up at him.

"He works...at the museum." "Which museum?" Penny asked.

"The one with all the bones," Jack said. "Dinosaur bones."

"The Field Museum," Mr. Kelley realized. Then, he cleared his throat. "How about going to pay your uncle a visit at his job? You think that would be all right?"

Jack cocked his head, as if thinking.

"Yeah," he finally decided. "I think that would be okay. As long as we had a ticket."

"We can get tickets," Penny said quickly. "Want to go now?"

"We can go now?" Jack sat up straight.

"Sure, you're done with your ice cream," Mr. Kelley said. "But I think we'd better ride the L." Jack's eyes went wide again.

"We're gonna ride the L?"

"Haven't you ever ridden the L?" Mr. Kelley asked.

"I...one time," Jack said. "But I was little, I don't remember."

"Well, come on, then," Penny smiled. "Give me that sticky paw."

Jack giggled, then hopped out of the booth after her, taking her hand. Mr. Kelley escorted them out and down the street once more, heading for the nearest L station. They climbed the stairs, Mr. Kelley paid for their tokens, and they climbed aboard the rattling elevated train. Mr. Kelley stood and held onto the bar while Penny found the one free seat, and pulled Jack into her lap.

The ride lasted several minutes, and nobody spoke. All the other people in the train either read the newspapers, books, or just dozed. Jack watched raptly out the windows, attentive and serious. Penny studied Mr. Kelley as Mr. Kelley studied Jack. Not for the first time, she marveled at how unconsciously handsome her boss was—especially in unguarded moments when that hard façade of his dropped a little. Moments like this one.

At last, they arrived at their station stop and got off the train. A breath of fresh, watery air greeted them, and they made their way along the sparkling waterfront toward the majestic Field Museum of Natural History. It was a huge, white, Grecian building with four massive pillars in front, and majestic stairs leading up to the front entrance. Jack started skipping with excitement as they approached, and sometimes Penny could hardly hold onto him.

He danced up the stairs as Penny and Mr. Kelley traipsed up with him, and when they entered the impressive marble lobby, they stood in line with other patrons to buy their tickets. After Mr. Kelley had bought them, they stepped through the main doors into the grand hall, where soaring ceilings enshrined the giant skeletons of several long-necked dinosaurs, and an impressive woolly mammoth. Jack immediately broke away from Penny and dashed up to the dinosaurs, beaming up at them in delight. Penny and Mr. Kelley followed, and, to Penny's relief, Mr. Kelley did not break into the boy's rapture for several minutes. And when he did, he was gentle.

"Where does your uncle work, Jack?"

Jack took a long time to answer. Finally, though, he wrenched his attention down from the towering head of the extinct lizard, and turned to Mr. Kelley.

"I think..." he frowned. "I think he's with the mummies."

"The mummies," Penny said. "In the Ancient Egypt section."

"I'll go find us a map," Mr. Kelley said, and strode off to find a kiosk. While he was gone, Penny talked with Jack about the dinosaurs, and read him the plaque about the three skeletons that stood before them.

Soon, Mr. Kelley came back, bearing a map of the museum.

"All right, it's through here and in the lower level," he said. "Let's go."

They did. And Penny sensed that Mr. Kelley would have liked to take a direct route to that portion.

However, they were walking with a little boy. A curious little boy who was growing increasingly more charming with every passing moment. As a result, Penny and Mr. Kelley were— rather willingly—pulled into various exhibits along the way, from relics of Mongolia to fossils of sea creatures, to animals of the African plains. A good hour later, they finally arrived at the Ancient Egypt section: a portion constructed to look like an Egyptian village, complete with hieroglyphics on the walls. Not many people explored this area, and so the three of them crept from quiet room to quiet room, admiring the mummy coffins and furniture and treasure. Jack perused everything with intense fascination. Even Mr. Kelley began to take an interest, pausing to read the plaques and bend close to study the relics. Once, when he caught Penny looking at him, he shrugged.

"I paid half a dollar a piece for us to get in here," he said. "Might as well get my money's worth."

After a while, Penny realized they had combed the Ancient Egypt portion—and the only person working in the area was a woman in her forties who had only recently come back to the states from an excavation. Most definitely not Jack's uncle.

"Where do you suppose he could be, Jack?" Penny wondered. Jack lifted his shoulders.

"Maybe he's somewhere else in the museum?" he offered. "He doesn't just do Egypt. Sometimes he does other old things, like Romans and Greeks, I think."

"All right, let's head to Rome," Mr. Kelley suggested. And so they did.

They traipsed through all the ancient civilizations, learning about all the Caesars and gazing at their marble busts. They explored China and India, Peru and Australia. They got stuck for a long time in a long hall filled with stuffed snakes.

And all the while, though Penny enjoyed herself, a niggling and uncomfortable thought began to trouble her. One that she really didn't want to voice.

Then, all at once, they came to the very last exhibit: a white room devoted to American Indian art. Never once had Jack recognized a single person working in the whole museum—nor had anyone recognized him. And here, a very old man in a museum uniform walked toward them from the other side of the room and smiled.

"Museum closes in ten minutes, folks," he said.

"Oh...Thank you," Penny said, dismayed.

The old man left the room. Jack trailed forward—and Penny saw a slump in his shoulders. He approached one of the display cases. Penny could see his face through the glass as he gazed mournfully at a leather shield. For a long time, no one said anything.

"Is this what it's like?" Jack finally said, his voice trembling.

"Is this what what's like, sweetheart?" Penny asked.

"To have a Saturday with your mom and dad?" he whimpered.

And then, all of a sudden, he burst into tears.

Penny, shocked to her core, almost moved...

But before she could, Mr. Kelley strode across the room, swept the boy up into his arms and held him. Jack threw his arms around Mr. Kelley's neck and bawled into this shoulder.

"Hey, hey, hey, kid. Take it easy," Mr. Kelley soothed, patting his back. "What's the matter, huh? Where are your folks?"

"I ain't got no folks," Jack stammered haltingly. "Ain't got nobody. I'm at a stupid orphanage and I hate it!" And he broke out into another wail, burying his face into Mr. Kelley's neck. Penny pressed a hand to her heart. Mr. Kelley, brow twisting, held the boy tighter.

"Why do you hate it?" he asked. "Grown-ups pick on you there? Don't give you enough food?"

"No," Jack shook his head, sitting back and swiping at his face. "They don't pick on me..." Mr. Kelley dug out his handkerchief and wiped Jack's face.

"Got enough food there?"

"I guess," Jack whispered, lip trembling.

"Then what's the problem?" Mr. Kelley asked.

"I don't belong to nobody," Jack wept, more tears running down. "Nobody wants me. And I can't play catch, and the other boys think I'm stupid."

"I'll teach you to play catch," Mr. Kelley suddenly said.

Jack hiccupped, then stared at him through his tears.

"Huh?"

"I'll teach you to play catch," Mr. Kelly stated. "I played ball in college. I was a pitcher." "You were?" Jack said in astonishment.

"Yep. Almost got picked to play for the Cubs, but I went to the war instead," Mr. Kelley told

him. "Blew my shot. But I can still throw, and I can teach you. It's easy."

"Really?" Jack whispered—his eyes shining as if this were too good to be true.

"Honest. I swear," Mr. Kelley said solemnly. "You've got my word on it. I'll come by every Saturday afternoon and we can play in the alley. Okay?" Mr. Kelley slapped his back lightly. Jack managed a trembling smile.

"Okay."

"But I'm gonna need the address if I'm gonna find my way there," Mr. Kelley said.

"Saint...Francis Home for...Orphans and Foundlings," Jack supplied, rubbing at his face again.

"All right. They serve supper there?"

"Yeah," Jack nodded.

"Okay, let's get you home for supper then," Mr. Kelley adjusted his hold on him. "And who's in charge of that joint?"

"Mrs. Finnigan."

"Nice lady?"

"She's okay," Jack admitted.

"Okay, we'll talk to her when we get there, make sure it's okay that I come play ball," Mr.

Kelley assured him. "We'll work it all out. It'll be okay. Promise."

And with that, Mr. Kelley carried Jack out of the American Indian room toward the front of the museum, Penny following in silent wonder. When they'd almost reached the doors, Mr. Kelley glanced over at her.

"What?" he muttered. "Don't look at me like that."

But he was smiling. And Penny smiled, too.

CHAPTER FOUR: Nothing to Lose

DETECTIVE GABRIEL KELLEY usually liked the water. He'd been like a fish when he was a kid, splashing and then swimming in the cool waters of Lake Michigan every summer. He'd been on the swimming team in high school, and garnered several medals. He'd loved the way all the world above disappeared when he dived down low, and everything turned to flickering brilliance and rippling light. He enjoyed the way the water glided smoothly past his skin as he cut silently through it, speeding along like a torpedo.

He usually liked the water.

But not tonight.

Tonight, the black waters of Lake Michigan lay quiet and malevolent—black as ink, and silent as a secret. The occasional light from a rare lamppost reflected upon its eerie surface like murky candlelight. Gabriel sat at the front of the small motorboat, his hands tucked deep inside the pockets of his mack coat, his hat pulled down low to his eyebrows. He watched. And he waited.

Old John Greene, the owner of the boat and its pilot, sat just as silently back there at the wheel. Occasionally, he shifted nervously, but knew better than to call up to Gabriel to ask any questions. The sound of a voice, even a whispered one, could carry too easily over the mirror surface of the waters.

They'd been at this vigil for hours—floating just off shore by a deserted stretch of beach some distance from the city, on a completely dark boat. It had to be past three in the morning. Another detective would have already called it quits, and chalked it up to a false alarm. But Gabriel didn't move. He kept his eyes fixed on the nearby shore where he knew a small fishing dock stretched out into the water, watching for any sign of movement. Listening for any sound.

Then...

Gabriel frowned.

A low rumble broke the silence of the night.

He sat up. He sensed John Greene do the same.

In a few moments, a flicker of light appeared through the dense trees. The bouncing of headlights.

The next minute, Gabriel saw a car speed down the wooded passage and swerve along the road beside the beach, then drive directly onto the fishing dock. With a screech of brakes, it halted about halfway down.

Then, as Gabriel stared, unbreathing, two men leaped out of each side of the car. They both wore long coats and wide-brimmed hats, and the one from the passenger side hefted a large handgun. They swept around to the back of the car and heaved open the trunk. Then, the driver yanked a man out of the trunk.

A live man.

Gabriel's heart started beating fast.

He was a small man, and the driver hauled him around in front of the car. It looked like he was just wearing a shirt and trousers, no coat or hat. He clearly had his hands tied behind his back. And his muffled cries proved he'd been gagged. The passenger heaved something else out of the trunk: a very heavy bag, with ropes trailing from it. It looked like a bag of bricks.

The two men dragged the man and the bag to the end of the dock, where a single dock light barely illuminated their movements. As Gabriel stared, the driver held the man while the passenger tied the ropes of the bag tight around the man's chest and shoulders, and wrapped the excess around his neck. Though the man struggled, he couldn't fight his way free.

Then—

The driver and passenger picked up the heavy bag together, and flung it into the water. The victim was suddenly jerked off the dock and plunged below the surface with an awful splash.

The driver and passenger watched for a moment, then turned and jogged to the car. They got in, shut their doors, reversed off the bridge, and drove back up the road and into the woods.

"Go!" Gabriel barked.

The next second, John Greene fired up the boat engine. Gabriel switched on the brilliant floodlight mounted on the front, and the little boat sped forward. Gabriel steered the light, pointing it toward the end of the dock...

Where he could see bubbles rising to the surface.

"Hold, hold, hold!" Gabriel held up a hand. "Right here, that's good. Cut it!"

John Green cut the engine. Gabriel flung off his hat and coat, and pulled a long knife from his belt. He stood up and perched on the edge of the boat, taking several deep breaths as he stared right down at those bubbles...

Then dove off, straight into the black water.

As soon as he went under, he could see nothing. Just disorienting blackness everywhere.

However, he could feel the bubbles hitting his face. He had to dive straight down. So he did. He kicked hard, plunging down and down, searching with his hands rather than his eyes. The water became icy cold, and pushed on his ears and chest. He kicked again, harder.

It was deeper here than he had thought. He hadn't quite calculated enough breath. If he didn't find him in a matter of seconds, he would have to go back up and take another breath— His left hand bumped something. He snatched at it.

It was a shoe.

A man's shoe—on a foot.

Gabriel took firm hold of it and pulled himself downward. He felt the legs of the man, now, then his chest. He was still floating, his chest toward the surface, his arms twisted behind him and attached to that heavy load. The man was writhing and squirming, and his foot connected with Gabriel's shoulder. It almost knocked him loose.

He grabbed the man's right arm savagely, pulled himself down even further to get away from his feet...

And began sawing at the long rope that tied him to the bag.

It was a sharp knife. It didn't take long.

The next instant, the man was free.

Gabriel swooped an arm underneath the man's and wrapped it around his chest. Then, he gave several hard kicks and dragged him to the surface.

Their heads broke through the water. Gabriel took a hard gasp.

Mr. Greene grabbed hold of his shirt, but Gabriel pushed the stranger forward.

"Pull him up," he panted. "Take off his gag so he can breathe."

"Alrightee," Mr. Greene grunted, and hauled the stranger over the side and tugged off his gag.

The stranger began gagging and rasping, spitting out water and coughing. Mr. Greene then helped Gabriel up and into the boat. Gabriel, still breathing hard, sat down on a bench and pushed the hair out of his face. Mr. Greene set in to untie the stranger, and Gabriel studied him as best he could in this light.

He was indeed a very small, stocky man, mostly bald, with a mustache and large eyes. He wore a work shirt and slacks, and boots. All sopping wet of course. When Mr. Greene freed him, he threw himself back against the side of the boat, wide-eyed.

"Who...Who are you?" he yelped, still spitting water.

"I'm Detective Gabriel Kelley," Gabriel answered, picking up a towel and drying his face.

"Who are you?"

"I'm...I'm David Landon," the little man stammered. "You...You just saved my life!"

"Yes, I did," Gabriel sighed, nodding.

"Why?" Mr. Landon demanded.

"Apart from it being my duty as a good citizen?" Gabriel smiled wryly. "I want you to help me."

Mr. Landon looked rapidly between Mr. Greene and Gabriel, and swallowed.

"Help you? With what?"

"With bringing down Harry the Mask," Gabriel said, his smile disappearing as he stared straight at the man. "I'm going to bring you down to headquarters and get you some dry clothes. Want a cup of coffee?"

Mr. Landon didn't answer, but Mr. Greene pulled out a thermos and poured him the coffee. Mr. Landon took it in trembling hands, while Mr. Greene sat back down behind the wheel and turned on the engine. In a matter of seconds, he had wheeled the little boat around, and they were speeding back toward one of the city police docks.

Back at headquarters, Gabriel left Mr. Landon with a couple officials while he went up to his office to change clothes. He always kept a spare suit in there, just in case the one he was wearing got messy and he didn't have time to drag himself all the way back to the apartment. He left the wet one on a hanger, on a hook on the wall near Penny's desk. She would take to the laundry tomorrow morning.

After he'd cleaned up as much as possible, he went back downstairs to find Mr. Landon sitting in a room at a table wrapped in a thick towel, cradling a cup of coffee—but looking white as a sheet.

Gabriel went in, and smiled at him.

"Hiya, Mr. Landon. Feeling any better?"

"Like a drowned rat," Mr. Landon shivered, pulling the coffee cup closer. "Can't I go home?

I've gotta get out of these wet clothes."

"Why don't you wait to hear what I have to say first," Gabriel offered, pulling out the chair across from him and sitting down. "I've been given authority to offer you a deal."

"Deal? What deal?" Mr. Landon said shrilly. "I haven't done anything wrong."

"Nobody says you have. I'm not accusing you of anything," Gabriel assured him. "What I'm offering is protection."

"Protection?" Mr. Landon eyed him. "In exchange for what?"

"We want you to testify against Harry the Mask."

Mr. Landon stared at him.

"Testify?" he whispered. "Against that gangster? The gangster who just now tried to have me killed?"

"That's exactly what I want you to do," Gabriel said firmly. "He attempted to murder you.

Why did he do that?"

"Because I was an idiot, that's why!" Mr. Landon shot back.

Gabriel frowned.

"What do you mean?"

Mr. Landon raked a hand across his bald head.

"I run an ice and coal business, okay? Makes pretty good money. Some of Harry's men came in the other day and offered me protection in exchange for a cut of my business." He shivered again, and shook his head. "Like a fool, I stood on principle. Told them I didn't need any help from the mob, thank you very much. They left, then. I suppose they might have left me alone if I'd just minded my own business—but then I shot my mouth off to my neighbors. Told them they ought to just tell Harry and his guys to take a hike, too. Next thing I know, they're dragging me out of my office in the middle of the night and throwing me in the trunk of a car." Mr. Landon gave him a hunted look. "And you want me to testify against a man like that?"

"I need you to, Mr. Landon," Gabriel leaned forward. "Otherwise, he's just going to keep doing this to more innocent people. You have to be brave."

"Brave!" Mr. Landon suddenly barked. "Brave—really? That's what they told my brother so he'd go enlist and get all shot up over there in France! Brave?" Now, he leaned toward Gabriel. "You ain't got no family, do you, mister detective?"

"I've got a mom and dad," Gabriel answered. Mr. Landon shook his head.

"Yeah, but you ain't got no wife or kids, huh? Nobody depending upon you for protection and provision, huh?"

Gabriel's jaw tightened. He didn't have to answer—Mr. Landon saw the truth.

"Yeah, I thought so," Mr. Landon sat back. "Well I've got a wife and three kids. They all depend on me, see? She needs her husband, they need their dad. I feed 'em, I put clothes on 'em. I'm supposed to keep 'em safe! Now how could I do that if I testify against this gangster? What, you're gonna put me away in some safehouse? What about my wife and kids? You gonna put all them in there, too? For how long? A year? Locked up in a hole, scared for our lives?" Mr. Landon leaned forward, his voice dropping. "And let's say you're an honest guy. Which I think you might be, by looking at you. And I really am grateful for what you did for me. But you and I both know..." His voice hardened. "This town is full of dirty cops. How do I know Harry the Mask won't pay off the guards and come strangle us all in our sleep?"

Gabriel clenched his teeth, staring back at him...

Unable to come up with an answer. Mr. Landon shook his head again.

"You wouldn't understand, that's why you asked me that question," Mr. Landon said. "You can afford to be brave. You've got nothing to lose."

Gabriel swallowed, the knife of that statement penetrating deep through his chest. He glanced down for a moment, then back up at Mr. Landon, ironing out his expression.

"What'll you do, then?"

Mr. Landon sat back, wrapping the towel tighter around himself.

"As soon as you guys let me loose, I'm going straight home," he said. "I'm packing up everything and getting my family out of this town tonight. We'll go south—I've got cousins in Kansas City. They can put us up for a little while. I imagine they need ice and coal in Kansas City, same as they do here."

"I'm sure they do," Gabriel said flatly, still watching him. "You sure I can't change your mind." "Nah," Mr. Landon said decisively. "Maybe if I was some single young man in need of a thrill. But I ain't. I've got a woman to protect, and kids. I've gotta think of them."

Gabriel left him then, and had the officers show him out. He even paid for his cab. And he watched as he drove away into the darkness, hearing his almost accusatory words reecho through his memory.

"You wouldn't understand, that's why you asked me that question. You can afford to be brave. You've got nothing to lose."

CHAPTER FIVE: Secret Mission

PENNY HATED DRIVING at night.

Especially alone, in Chicago.

The streetlights glared against the windshield and the windows, pedestrians became difficult to see, and blazing headlights seemed to appear around corners just to blind her.

Besides which, this wasn't her car.

She actually didn't have a car. She had her license, because her mother had insisted that if she was going to be living in a big city, she ought to be able to drive, even if she didn't own a car—that it was silly to handicap herself for no reason. And what if some emergency arose? Penny had to agree with that, but it didn't make it any more fun for her. Especially when she was driving the chief's car.

It was a black Oldsmobile, with a little frowning windshield and small windows. Extremely hard to maneuver in reverse. Not much better when driving forward.

Penny gritted her teeth and leaned forward, her gloved hands gripping the steering wheel as she peered out into the darkness. Occasionally, she glanced down into her lap at the sheet of paper where her directions had been written—though she had to time that carefully to match the occasions when she drove past a streetlamp, so she could actually see it. She had just taken turn number four. There were six more to go.

That is, if she could correctly read Mr. Kelley's handwriting.

She had to admit, she had gotten fairly good at deciphering his careless scrawl during these past two years she had worked for him. Most people couldn't read anything he wrote when he was in a hurry—it looked like some form of Arabic.

However, when he paused and gathered himself, and took the time to really craft a thoughtful note, his penmanship was beautiful. Penny remembered seeing it for the first time when he asked her to mail a letter to his mother—she had been astonished.

And pleased. She had been pleased.

These directions, however, had most certainly been written in a hurry. And they were difficult to make out, even for Penny.

"Turning right, turning right...here..." she muttered as she performed the turn, wincing. It took her down a darker, emptier road, and she sat up a little. Where was she...?

Wincing harder, she kept going, sharpening her attention for all the street signs she could see.

There, she made a turn at Euclid. There, another turn at Beecher. Another at Chaplin.

The roads became longer, the stops between them less frequent. The traffic thinner and thinner.

She even caught sight of a tree. Then another. Then two more.

She looked down at her directions. She only had one more turn.

At last, she swung to the left, her headlights bouncing through the darkness...

Into the dirt parking lot of an old gas station.

The pumps weren't lit, but the lights were on inside. Penny drew the car to a stop in front of the station, put it in park, and hesitated.

Was this the right place...?

She saw no movement from inside. Biting her lip, she turned off the engine, climbed out, and took the paper bag with her.

The slam of the car door seemed inordinately loud, and she flinched. Then, clearing her throat and straightening her jacket and hat, she strode up to the door of the gas station, pulled it open and stepped inside.

It smelled greasy, like bacon fat. A few shelves stood around, lined with auto parts, and others held snacks like nuts and dried fruits and candies. And there, at the far end, near the counter, stood her boss, Detective Kelley.

He still wore his coat and his hat, and he leaned on the counter, talking to the man who obviously owned the place: a pot-bellied gentleman with a stained shirt, a broad smile and a missing tooth in the front. Both men turned when she entered.

"Brought it?" Mr. Kelley called to her.

"Of course," she nodded quickly, coming up to him and handing him the bag. "Any way you could tell me what this is about?"

"Not right now," Mr. Kelley shook his head, peeking inside the bag. Then, he nodded and handed it to the other man. "There you go, Reggie. Whaddya say?"

Reggie eyed him, then took the bag in a meaty hand. He didn't draw out its contents, but reached inside and rifled through it, looking down inside carefully. He paused.

Then, he grinned and rolled the paper bag up tight.

"We've got a deal, my friend." And he reached into his apron pocket and handed Mr. Kelley an envelope.

"Thanks. Nice doing business with you," Mr. Kelley saluted him with the envelope.

"Have a nice night!" Reggie chuckled, as if something were very funny, and he turned to head through a back door.

"What's this all about?" Penny hissed. Mr. Kelley glanced at her.

"Can you be available tomorrow evening?" Her eyebrows raised.

"Um...yes?"

"Fine, thanks."

"Do you...need a ride back?" she asked, pointing with her thumb over her shoulder.

"No, I have a couple other people to see," he said. Then, he stopped and really looked at her.

"How was the drive? Have any trouble?"

"No," Penny said quickly, feeling herself blush. "No, not at all."

"Good." He smiled a little. "See you in the morning, Pen."

And with that, he strode past her and left the gas station.

Frowning hard, Penny eventually left too, but when she did, she didn't see him anywhere.

Sighing, she got back into the car, turned it on, and drove out of the parking lot.

What was Mr. Kelley up to? He had called her at her boarding house at eight o'clock at night, telling her to go to his office and retrieve a paper bag from inside his desk—but not to look inside it under any circumstances. Then, she was to find a set of written directions lying on the desk, and to take that with her. He had then instructed her to go down to the police chief's office, for he was still working, and tell him she needed to use his car to take something vital to Detective Kelley.

That had been the difficult bit, to be sure. The chief had not at all been inclined to loan out his car. The only reason he had probably consented was that Penny was known to be an honest girl and a hard worker, following her boss' instructions.

Now, though, Penny felt a little irritated. Perhaps more than that. She had expected to come in on an emergency, some sort of high stakes play. Instead, she'd seen a casual trade of some kind between a grimy gas station owner and a very casual detective who could easily have just been a customer.

What had Kelley handed him, anyway? A baloney sandwich?

Grinding her teeth, Penny got more and more irritated the longer she drove, until she finally reached the police station again.

"What was the big emergency?" the chief asked as she handed him back the keys. "You'll have to ask Mr. Kelley, sir," Penny answered, trying not to snap at him. "If you'll excuse me, I'm going home to bed."

It was eleven thirty by the time she finally climbed between the sheets.

But she was still mad.

The next morning, a Friday, Mr. Kelley didn't come in until half past ten. And he didn't say anything at all about the previous night's escapades. She glared at him each time he emerged from the office—but that wasn't often. And at about four o'clock, he strode out, grabbed his coat and hat, and turned briskly to her.

"Meet me downstairs at five, okay Pen?"

And without waiting for an answer, Mr. Kelley vanished through the door.

"Errrghh!" Penny snarled, thumping her hands on her typewriter and sitting back, crossing her arms. Infuriating man. Hadn't even given her the chance to bawl him out.

She finished up the rest of her work, still stewing and muttering to herself. Finally, the hands of the clock approached five, and she locked up the desk, put everything away, donned her own coat and hat and snatched her purse.

"Available this evening. Sure, what for? None of your business, I'm not telling you. Just be available," she mumbled as she headed down the hallway and descended the elevator.

She found him standing in the lobby, his hands in his pockets. She prepared a scathing frown, opened her mouth...

And he smiled at her.

Her words flew away.

It was his real smile—the one that made him look unexpectedly handsome. Just like Rudolph Valentino.

She almost tripped.

"Hiya, Penny. Ready to go?"

"Um...Yes?" she stammered.

"C'mon."

And together, they left the office building, and headed down the street. Again, Mr. Kelley took the outside position, closest to the street. They maneuvered down to the L station, climbed the stairs, and Mr.

Kelley paid for two. Penny watched him carefully, but he just whistled a tune to himself—and once, he smiled at her again. Which completely disarmed her.

What was going on?

They climbed aboard the L train, and Mr. Kelley found a place for them both to sit down. Penny blushed again. Her side was pressed against his, and she could smell his cologne. She lifted her chin, and tried to show nothing on her face. The train started off.

It made several stops, and each time, more and more people piled on. And as Penny watched, she noticed more and more kids, especially boys. And then three or four of them came on, each toting a baseball glove. It dawned on her.

"Ah. Everyone's going to the ballpark," she smiled.

Mr. Kelley glanced at her. She hadn't realized he heard her.

And he kept looking at her. So she kept talking.

"My dad took my brother and I to a game when I was twelve," she said. "We sat all the way up in the cheap seats, but we could still see the action. Dad bought us a box of cracker jacks. Steve and I fought over the toy inside." She chuckled. "They played the Yankees, and the Cubs won four to three.

The place went wild." Her smile broadened. "One of the best days I've ever had."

"Yeah," Mr. Kelley murmured. She looked at him. He met her eyes briefly...

Then looked away, turning his attention to a man reading a newspaper across the way. Penny said no more.

More and more people climbed on, until even the standing room was packed to the gills. It became hot and stifling, and Penny wondered how she and Mr. Kelley would ever work their way through all these people when it came time to get off.

But they didn't get off. Mr. Kelley never made a move to rise when the train halted. At last, it sped off one more time...

And then the call came through:

Station stop: Wrigley Field.

The doors opened. All the people poured out.

Mr. Kelley got to his feet and held out his arm to her.

"Hold onto me, Penny," he instructed. "Don't want to lose you."

Confounded, Penny stood up and took his arm, and together they left the train amongst the jostling crowd. They left the platform and stepped out onto the street right in front of the towering brick stadium, and joined the line of people...

"What are we doing?" Penny asked suddenly. "Are we...Are we actually going to...a ballgame?"

Mr. Kelley reached inside his pocket...

And drew out two tickets. He handed one to Penny.

Her heart skipped a beat as she read it.

CHICAGO CUBS VS NEW YORK YANKEES – FRIDAY, 7PM – BOX 6

"Box seats?" she gasped, turning to him. "How...why did you get these?"

"I got a tip that Harry might send a couple goons to sit in the box over," Mr. Kelley said lightly.

"Don't think they'll do anything, but I'd like to keep my eye on them."

"But these are expensive!" Penny cried. "How did you get them?"

"Reggie would have given me one ticket for twenty bucks. But for these, I had to give him my Babe Ruth signed baseball."

Penny gaped at him.

"Why?"

He smiled at her again—quietly.

"Because I wanted two."

Penny had no idea what to say. But she couldn't stop herself from smiling stupidly.

The line traveled quickly, and they handed their tickets to the man, who tore them and then handed one piece back. Then, Mr. Kelley led her to the box seats: perfect seats right next to the first base line. Penny could see everything—practically the stitches on the uniforms.

They settled into the seats, Penny marveling at the happy crowds, the teams warming up, the slap of the ball into the gloves, the organ playing its carnival tunes, the shouts of the vendors...

One such vendor in his white uniform and cap, carrying his tray in front of him, began marching up and down the aisle nearest them. Then, to Penny's surprise—and she blushed again—Mr. Kelley turned to her.

"Hey, Pen," he nodded toward the vendor. "Want some crackerjacks?"

CHAPTER SIX: Insurance Policy

IF THERE WAS ONE THING that made the hair on the back of Detective Gabriel Kelley's neck stand on end, it was the smell of a speakeasy.

It wasn't just the odor of all kinds of bootlegged hooch mixed together into one overpowering cocktail. It was also the noxious clouds of cigarette smoke swirling alongside waves of cheap perfume.

Whenever he took a deep breath of that, he knew he was literally smelling trouble.

He stepped through the door into the low-lit room and handed the attendant his coat and hat, then helped his date off with her long, white fur coat.

Her perfume, in contrast, was not cheap. In fact, it was Chanel Number 5.

Nothing but the best for Miss Vivian Hargate.

She was a sleek and ravishing blonde with elegant curves, now hugged by a silk, scarlet dress with a tasteful but plunging neckline. Tiny diamonds sparkled around her long, white neck, and by her rosy cheeks. She had a pert, saucy red mouth; large, sultry blue eyes and arched eyebrows—a glance that could kill a man...

Or make him go weak at the knees and melt right to the floor.

After Gabriel handed her coat off, Vivian lightly took his arm and strolled alongside him further into the room, every movement of her body like liquid. A diamond bracelet twinkled on her wrist. Gabriel watched as she scanned the room, half a smile on that inviting mouth, her intelligent eyes picking out the familiar faces in the dark.

"See anyone we know?" Gabriel muttered, scanning the room too.

"Oh, Gabe, let's not worry about that tonight, okay?" she sighed, glancing at him. "Let's just relax and let off some steam. I think we've both earned it."

"I'm not sure about that," he answered. "But we can get a table and order some drinks." Just then, the head waiter approached them, bowed, and smiled at Vivian.

"Miss Hargate, so nice to see you again," he said. "Would you like your usual table?"

"Yes, please Frankie," she winked at him. "If you'd be so kind."

"It would be my pleasure," he said. "Follow me."

He led the way to a corner booth that sat thick in darkness, with only a small candle sitting in the center for illumination. Vivian slid languidly into it, and turned a beckoning smile to Gabriel. He sat down next to her, unbuttoning his jacket. Vivian draped herself against his side, and again his senses filled with Chanel No. 5.

"What would you like to drink?" Frankie asked.

"My friend knows what I like," Vivian said, resting her chin on Gabriel's shoulder.

"Two martinis, please," Gabriel told the waiter. "Both with one olive."

"Right away, sir," Frankie replied, and turned away. Gabriel again looked around the room...

"This is my favorite booth," Vivian purred in his ear. "No one can see us."

He turned his head to her...

She met his eyes for a moment—dusky and warm in the candlelight—before she closed the distance and kissed him. Gabriel shut his eyes. She slowly wrapped her hand around his neck as she gently, playfully kissed him...

And he kissed her in reply, taking deep breaths of that elegant perfume. Soon, he slipped his arm around her waist and pulled her closer against him, and her right hand came up to take hold of his tie. Their kisses deepened, and began to quicken...

A soft sound. Gabriel opened his left eye and saw that the martinis had magically appeared at their table. He turned back to Vivian...

Her nose touched his, and a soft smile touched her mouth.

He kissed her again, harder this time, sighing and surrendering his vigil for the time being. He wasn't much of one for bootlegged hooch, anyway. And it was easy to forget about the rest of the world with Vivian in his arms.

Several minutes later, however, he had to wrench his attention away—because a stir rippled through the speakeasy. Both he and Vivian turned toward the entrance, frowning... As three men entered.

Gabriel recognized them right away.

Haystack, Philly Cat, and Duke.

Haystack was a large, square gangster who favored a black and white zoot suit, and had strawlike yellow hair combed straight down all around his small head. And his fists seemed quite a bit bigger than his head.

Philly Cat was small and lean, with a perpetual smirk, a pencil mustache and a fine tailored suit, with a purple silk tie. His black fedora always sat cocked to the right side. He smoked thin cigarettes, which he lit with a silver, engraved lighter. He was a dangerous gambler.

Duke was a broad-shouldered, handsome man who definitely carried an air of aristocracy.

Brown hair, dark eyes—a classy wardrobe that was never overstated, and a face like Clark Gable.

They were three of Harry the Mask's closest friends.

Slowly, Gabriel withdrew his arms from around Vivian, and got to his feet.

"I think I'd rather have wine," Gabriel said, buttoning his coat. "You want something else, baby?"

"Maybe a little champagne," she smiled, smoothing her hair.

"Okay. I'll be right back."

Gabriel turned and maneuvered around the crowded tables toward the bar, keeping an eye on the three gangsters as he did. Those men nonchalantly moved to the bar also, chatting with Frankie as they did. Tommy, the bartender, turned around and asked them what they wanted. They each ordered their signature drinks: Haystack wanted beer, Philly Cat wanted whiskey, and Duke ordered red wine.

Gabriel kept those men to his right, and four other patrons between him and them, as he sidled up to the bar. However, he knew what would happen after Tommy served them and came to him.

And indeed, his prediction came true. After Tommy handed out the drinks to the three gangsters and approached him, he beamed a roguish smile. He was a handsome Italian man with slick black hair—and he looked dangerous, too. He probably was.

"Well, if it isn't our old friend Detective Kelley," he declared, resting his hands on the bar.

"Gonna haul us all in, copper? This some kinda raid?"

"I'm off duty tonight, Tommy," Gabriel answered. "I'm here with a lady friend."

"Aha, I see," Tommy winked at him. "Then what can I get for you and the lady?"

"Kelley? Gabriel Kelley?"

Gabriel turned at the sound of Philly Cat's voice. All three gangsters were looking down the bar at him now. Philly cat, as usual, smirked at him. Haystack just frowned dully—also as usual—and Duke scrutinized him. Gabriel nodded coolly, then turned back to Tommy.

"I'd like a cabernet sauvignon, and a glass of champagne, thanks Tommy."

"Certainly," Tommy turned around to pour the drinks.

Gabriel then sensed the gangsters slowly muscle their way closer to him, Philly Cat in the lead, until they hovered all around him. Philly Cat, just to his right, leaned his elbow on the bar and puffed at his cigarette.

"So, we're supposed to believe that you're just...what, out for a night on the town?" Philly Cat blew smoke in Gabriel's face. Gabriel gave him a glance, bored.

"I don't care what you believe, Cat," he said. "It's really none of your business."

"Oh, isn't it?" Philly Cat countered, his eyes flashing. "You threaten our boss' life, and you think you can just walk around on our turf all friendly-like, no problems?"

"You have to admit, it's a bit troublesome for us, Mr. Kelley," Duke added smoothly, coming around to Gabriel's left side, though not so close, and much more casual. However, Gabriel could feel Haystack's hulking presence right behind him.

"After all, we've got our orders," Philly Cat said quietly, ice entering his tone. "If we can make it look like an accident...we're supposed to. See?"

Gabriel's jaw tightened.

"Is that so?" he raised an eyebrow at Philly Cat. "He's got a hit out on me now, huh?"

"You do understand, Mr. Kelley," Duke said placidly. "Business is business."

"Yeah, sure," Gabriel answered, steeling his spine. "All in a day's work."

"See, he understands," Duke smiled politely—and glanced up at Haystack.

Two massive hands landed on Gabriel's shoulders, grabbed his coat—

"Tommy, sweetheart!" came a cheerful, musical voice...

And Vivian Hargate sauntered up to the bar.

Haystack instantly let go of Gabriel. Gabriel turned...

It was as if a magic spell had descended upon the gangsters. They stood, stunned to the floor, as Vivian looked from one to the other of them, her lips parted in an almost smile, her sultry eyes glancing each one up and down.

Haystack backed up, bewildered. Philly Cat cleared his throat, straightened and adjusted his tie.

Only Duke remained where he was...

But he softened, and gave her a winning smile.

"Good evening, Miss Hargate," he greeted her warmly. "How are you tonight?"

"Very well, thank you William," she beamed at him...

And Gabriel sensed Philly Cat's legs go weak.

Then, Vivian put on a playfully inquisitive expression.

"Are you boys having a drink together?" she looked saucily at Duke. "I believe that's my champagne, there."

"Oh, is it?" Philly cat said quickly, turning and picking it up off the bar, then presenting it to her as if she were a princess. "Here you are, Miss Hargate."

She laughed, and it rang like a shimmering bell.

"Thank you, Bobby," she winked at him. Then, a marvelous idea obviously occurred to her. "Why don't we all sit down and have a drink together, and talk about the races? I'm dying to hear about anything to do with horses!"

"Sure, okay," Haystack finally spoke up in his deep rumble. Then, as if surprised at himself, he looked at his companions...

Who agreed—also to their surprise.

However, when Vivian led Gabriel back to the booth, and asked Frankie to bring three more chairs and more drinks, the gangsters settled in with jovial and easy attitudes, compliantly discussing horse racing—all eyes on the siren in the scarlet dress.

True to form, they were willing to forget the violence of their jobs—and even their orders—if it meant basking in the radiant glow of Vivian Hargate's glances and musical laughter for a few hours.

Gabriel wasn't surprised. He'd known it would happen if he got in a pinch.

And he also knew the feeling.

CHAPTER SEVEN: A Shot in the Dark

CHICAGO, 1931

Gabriel Kelley clenched his teeth, gripping the handle of his revolver as the cold night air blew in through the broken window. He took a deep breath and relaxed his jaw.

"All right, Harry. You've got two choices. You can leave here on your feet...or in a body bag." Hoarse chuckling echoed from the darkness of the opposite corner, near the half open window. Through it, the skyline of Chicago flickered. High wind whistled through the teeth of the shattered glass. They were four stories up.

"Or what, Gabe?" Harry retorted, his speech slightly distorted, as always. "You'll shoot me? It's kinda dark over here. Might hit your pretty secretary."

A scuffling sound issued, and a sharp, female whimper.

Penny.

Something tightened hard inside Gabriel's chest. He narrowed his eyes and steadied his gun. "I don't need to see you, Harry," he answered coldly. "I'd know you anywhere. I could hit you in the pitch black, right between the eyes."

Harry laughed again, rough and crackling—then broke into his characteristic cough. For an instant, Gabriel hoped Penny might take advantage of the momentary weakness and wriggle free of his grasp—

A sharp fracas in the blackness, and Penny yelped again—then thudded back against the wall.

"Nice try, sweetheart," Harry snarled. "But you've got to be quicker."

"Let her go, Harry," Gabriel barked. "Let her go, and let's talk like men."

"Ah, that's very interesting," Harry snorted. "Appealing to my sense of honor, huh? Just like you did when we were down in those trenches together, huh? Knee deep in filthy water, sucking in mustard gas? Getting our faces shot off?" Just then, Harry shifted closer to the window, where a shaft of light illuminated what was left of his face.

Harry Holliday had once been an extraordinarily handsome man. Carelessly good-looking, tall and classy, with blond hair and a neat, stylish mustache. A dashing smile, and charming blue eyes.

Until a German bullet had met with his right cheekbone, and torn off a great deal of his flesh. Now, Harry wore a piece of piece of plastic roughly resembling a human face, covering the bleached scarring of his cheek and nose. But his right eye leered, half blind, and the corner of his mouth twisted.

Gabriel pushed down the flicker of horror that still haunted him every time he saw his old comrade now.

"I'm appealing to the man I know you are," Gabriel answered instead. "The good man I knew before the war."

"That man died in France," Harry shot back. "He should have, anyway. Instead, you dragged me back to the hospital where some ham-fisted veterinarian could try to put my mug back together like some demented Humpty Dumpty. And then you only got shot in the leg. Got sent home at the same time as me, as if our wounds were the same!" Harry's voice shook. "And when Vivian took one look at me, she screamed. Screamed like one of those dames in a scary picture show. Wouldn't even touch me—the man she was supposed to marry. Nah, wouldn't come near me. Who did she run to instead? Who did my gorgeous, knockout blonde fiancée run to? You. You lucky son of a gun." Harry snarled another laugh. "You should have let me drown in that sewage."

"To be honest, I wish I had," Gabriel answered, his face heating. "Rather than watch what you've been doing these past few years. You and your gang terrorize this city—there's no law and order, not anymore.

Ordinary folks are afraid to walk the streets. You've turned the place into a wcesspool with your gambling dens and your whorehouses and your speakeasies."

"To each his own, Gabe," Harry answered. "Ain't my fault we wound up on opposite teams, here. Remember, I offered you a job."

"Yeah. As a dirty cop," Gabriel's eyes narrowed. He stepped forward, and his shoes crunched on broken glass.

"Take one more step, and I'll break her neck," Harry warned, ice cold. "You know I will." Penny whimpered again. Gabriel stopped, his heart doing a flip. He searched through the darkness—but he still couldn't see her, and could only find the edge of Harry's nightmarish mask. He could tell, though, that Harry had tight hold of Penny from behind, and that she was gagged. He didn't dare make any fast moves.

"All right, what do you want, Harry?" Gabriel demanded. "What do you want in exchange for Penny?"

"What do you think I want, my friend?" Harry answered. "You're the head of the detective division that's making my life a living hell. You're destroying my business, scaring off my high paying customers. I want you to lay off."

"Lay off?" Gabriel repeated, frowning.

"You heard me," Harry said. "Lay off. Turn off the heat. Let us breathe a little. If you do, I'll see to it that it's worth your while. I know you're sick of living in that broom closet you call an apartment, listening to the L rattle by your face all night long. Let me make stuff easier for you. You scratch my back, I'll scratch yours."

"So you're back to asking me if I wanna dance with the devil," Gabriel growled.

"No, I'm asking if you finally wanna be reasonable," Harry countered. "Or...if you'd rather use that body bag you mentioned for this little lady instead."

"You think I'm going to call off the hunt for you and your boys," Gabriel growled. "Oh, I know you will, Gabe," Harry smirked. "One way or another."

"What makes you so sure?" Gabriel wanted to know.

"You'll come around, after you've had a bit to think about it," Harry assured him. "Say goodnight, copper."

Gabriel's eyes flashed—but he felt the presence behind him too late.

The next second, something hard and cold cracked him across the head, and everything went black.

Gabriel gasped. His head jerked up...

He groaned, wincing. Something hot ran down his forehead. It had to be blood.

He squeezed his eyes open, fighting dizziness, and tried to figure out where he was.

A murky, damp scent surrounded him. He felt his arms tied behind him to some kind of metal grate. He stood on a narrow stone lip. And just in front of him, down a few feet, lay a pool of quietly restless black water, which reflected the faint light from a grated manhole cover far overhead. He had to be down in the sewers.

A low rumble of thunder sounded. And then, with a slow, metallic tapping, it began to rain. The droplets fell down through the overhead grate, and dotted the pool before him.

"Kelley?"

Gabriel's head came around at the sound of the woman's voice.

"Penny?" he gasped. And when he finally got his eyes to focus, he could see her.

She stood off to his left, still wearing the same red polka dotted dress he'd seen her in when he had left the office earlier that day. She'd been seated behind the desk then, busily typing, her reading glasses perched on her pretty nose, her large brown eyes focused on her work. Her auburn hair had been pinned back neatly, her comely mouth set in concentration. But when he'd offered her an absentminded "'Night, Pen," as he walked past, she had looked up, given him her beautiful smile, and replied, "Goodnight, Mr. Kelley."

Now, though, her cute dress was stained, and her hair hung around her pale face. Her large brown eyes searched him, her brow furrowed tightly.

"Are you okay?" Gabriel asked over the patter of the rain, his voice echoing in their damp, circular prison.

"Yes, I'm all right," she answered, but she shivered.

"Did Harry hurt you?" Gabriel pressed.

"Well. His thugs didn't exactly use kid gloves when they found me at the office," she answered grimly. She paused, and her voice changed as she gazed at him. "Are you all right? It looks as though you're bleeding."

"Yeah. My head feels like it's been run over by an ice truck," he muttered, screwing his eyes shut before opening them again and looking at her.

"I'm sorry," Penny said. "I saw the man come up behind you with a billy club, but I couldn't make a sound. Harry was choking me."

The thunder rumbled again, and the rain increased. It dripped down the stone walls, and shimmered across the pool of water. Gabriel's dark hair got wet, and so did his brown suit. Soon, he would start shivering, too.

He gazed across at Penny, his heart sinking. He heaved a sigh, his eyebrows drawing together.

"I'm sorry I got you into this mess, Penny."

She watched him through the rain.

"Did you get me into this mess?"

"Yeah, I guess I did," he muttered. "It's my fault—I've been tangling with Harry all this time. I guess he was bound to..." He trailed off, suddenly afraid of what he had been about to say.

"This isn't your fault, Mr. Kelley," Penny finally said. "I know who I work for, and I know what kind of business he's in. I'm more than willing to take responsibility for myself."

"Yeah, well I'm not," Gabriel retorted. "What happens when this drain starts filling up with water? It's bound to—see how high the wet spot comes up? It's by your shoulder." A hole opened up inside him as he gazed across at her. "How well can you tread water, Pen?"

"I can't really swim," she said wryly. "My mother didn't think it was ladylike."

Gabriel swore, and pulled at the ropes.

"Even if I had my pocketknife, I couldn't get to it," he gritted. "And I'm sure Harry searched me."

"Are you tied up?" Penny asked suddenly.

"Yeah, they've got me pretty well hog tied," he muttered, pulling again at the wet ropes. "I'm not," she gasped. "I've just been afraid to try to walk on this slippery little ledge." Gabriel looked up at her quickly. She leaned toward him, her brow furrowed earnestly.

"You said you can't swim?" he asked.

"No, I can't," she shook her head.

"Then stay right there," he ordered. "I'll figure a way out of these myself."

For several minutes, he continued to wrestle with the ropes, chafing and twisting his skin as he did. He bared his teeth, trying to wriggle this way and that—but Harry had tied an expert knot.

"Are you sure you don't want help?" Penny called.

"Stay there," Gabriel said through his teeth. "If you fell in, I couldn't help you."

A deep sound issued from somewhere far up some darkened tunnel. A deep, heavy sloshing sound.

"What's that?" Penny whispered.

"Dunno," Gabriel murmured back, frowning.

But three seconds later, they got their answer.

The water at their feet began to shift and shiver, its edges rippling...

And the level began to rise.

"Kelley!" Penny cried, pressing herself back against the wall. "The rain water's coming in!" Gabriel's heart began to pound as he wrenched at the ropes. The water spilled up over the lip and doused his feet. It was ice cold.

"Mr. Kelley, I've got to come help you," Penny insisted frantically.

"Don't you dare," he snapped.

"I can't swim!" she yelped. "Who's going to help me if you stay tied up?"

He had no answer for that. And as the water swallowed his ankles, a strange panic began rising within him.

Nightmarish images flashed through his mind—gas-drenched memories of slogging through wretched puddles of mud that filled the trenches, machine-gun fire rattling overhead as the rain poured down in torrents, like waterfalls of sludge. Woe betide the man who lost his footing and fell down to tangle with the limbs of the dead men lost beneath the water...

"I'm coming to you, Mr. Kelley." Penny's voice cut through the haze and his head came up. He saw her then, edging her way along the ledge, the water up to her calves.

"Penny, be careful," Gabriel ordered. "Go slowly."

She didn't answer, just kept her palms and back pressed against the wall, her eyes fixed on the water at her feet.

The water began to foam. With a frigid gush, a new wave washed in, and suddenly the level rose to up past their knees.

"Good gosh, this is cold," Penny said through her teeth.

"Just concentrate on where you're putting your feet," Gabriel reminded her. "Don't think of anything else."

She nodded absently, still edging toward him. The water began to swirl fitfully, and somehow, in no time at all, it rolled around Penny's hips.

"You're almost here, grab hold of me," Gabriel said, leaning toward her. "Penny—"

The water surged—

And Penny's left foot slipped.

She yelped—and tumbled into the water.

"Penny!" Gabriel shouted, but his voice was drowned out by the terrific splash.

Immediately, Penny surfaced, floundering and gasping.

"Penny! Penny, grab my ankle!" Gabriel called, bending his knees and sticking his left foot out as far as he could, his arms wrenched upward behind him. Sputtering and dipping beneath the water,

Penny flailed toward him once, twice— Her fingers snatched his pantleg.

"Hold on!" he gritted, pulling her toward him. "Keep hold of me!"

Groaning, he dragged her toward him and managed to stand upright again, Penny latching onto his calf, coughing.

"Climb up here, Pen," he urged. "Grab the edge and pull yourself up—"

A gurgling roar flooded the chamber...

And a huge wave engulfed them.

It struck Gabriel back against the wall, nearly driving the air from his lungs. Penny tore loose from his leg.

He forced his eyes open, but couldn't see anything. The black water now covered his head. He thrashed against the ropes, twisting with all his might, pulling and tugging until he felt he

almost tore his hands off. He kicked against the grate, he bared his teeth...

Penny was down here somewhere—she was down here, and she was drowning—

He felt something.

Something took hold of his left arm.

A hand.

Gabriel jerked, but he still couldn't see.

The hand became two hands, and they worked their way down his arm and found the ropes.

Penny!

He went still, and slackened his pull on the ropes. He felt her prying at the ropes as the side of her body bumped against his.

Gabriel's chest started to burn, his lungs threatening to burst. He hadn't had a chance to take a breath before the wave came. Had Penny?

Her quick fingers pulled and worked at the ropes. He could feel them—but he couldn't tell if she was making any progress. Once, twice, she tugged hard—and he could tell she was fighting against being pulled to the surface.

C'mon, Penny, let me go, he wanted to scream. Let me go and get up to the air...!

She pulled again. A large bubble of air escaped from her mouth.

Penny...!

Suddenly, the ropes came loose.

Shocked, Gabriel pulled his freed arms forward—

Then, he turned and snatched at Penny.

He wrapped his arm beneath her left and up across her chest, then kicked hard against the stone. He pumped hard, carrying her with him through the surging water, fighting the urge to open his mouth and gasp.

His right hand struck something—something metal protruding from the wall.

A ladder.

He grabbed it, scrambling to hold on when his hand was slick, and pulled up— His head broke the surface. So did Penny's.

They gasped desperately, water streaming off their faces. Now, the rain poured down on top of them.

"Penny...Pen, grab the ladder," he rasped, spitting out water and shoving her upward. Shakily, her hands slapped down on the rungs, and she started pulling herself up. Gabriel reached down and pulled off her shoes and let them sink, so she could get a more secure foothold. Then, he climbed up right behind her, his hands by her ankles. They clawed their way up the cold, wet ladder toward the grate, Gabriel blinking against the downpour. Then, Penny reached the grate, and reached up with her right hand. She pushed against it, and it groaned.

"I...I can't, Mr. Kelly," she panted. "It's too heavy, I can't lift it..."

Grunting, Gabriel put his left hand on the back of her leg and worked his way up the ladder beside her, wrapping his arm around her waist.

"Hang on, don't let me fall," he managed.

"Okay," she shivered, gripping the ladder hard. He held tight to her, wrapped his right leg around the ladder, and reached up to shove on the grate. And with a roar of effort, he finally slid it aside enough for them to slip through.

"Go on, go on," he gasped, lifting Penny past him. She climbed up and scrambled out, and he followed her. She knelt down and gave him her hand, and helped him up through the hole.

The next moment, they got to their feet in the middle of an alley filled with trash cans, the rain pouring all around them. A weak streetlight cast everything in a yellow glow. Gabriel took hold of Penny again, and hurried her into a deep doorway that offered a little protection from the deluge.

"Are you all right?" Gabriel panted, taking her by the shoulders.

And to his great surprise—she laughed.

It rang through the alley and bounced off the stones. He could see her by the light of the lamp: her hair soaking wet, her brown eyes even larger—and sparkling as she laughed.

"Well," she chuckled. "You certainly know how to show a girl a good time."

"Ha," he barked in amazement, raking a hand through his dark, wet hair. "You're some dame." "Thank you, I suppose," she answered, wrapping her arms around herself. "A dame without her new shoes!"

"We've got to get you out of this rain," Gabriel suddenly realized. "Come on." And without asking her, he bent down and easily picked her up, and carried her out of the alley. She didn't object— she knew what kind of metal and broken glass lay strewn around on the ground.

Once they reached the main street, he tucked her under an awning again while he stepped out into the downpour to hail a cab. It took several minutes, but finally one splashed through the puddle in the gutter and squeaked to a halt. Gabriel dashed back to Penny, picked her up again and carried her to the cab, set her down, opened the door and ushered her in. Then, he climbed in after her and shut the door.

At long last, the pounding sound of water ceased. He let out a long sigh, swiped the water out of his face and pushed his hair back. Out of the corner of his eye, he saw Penny doing the same.

"Ain't you two ever heard of the latest invention, the umbrella?" quipped the high-pitched voice of the driver.

"Left it at the office," Gabriel muttered.

"I guess so!" the driver huffed. "And letting your missus half drown? What kinda guy are ya?" "She's not my wife," Gabriel snapped.

Penny went still, and glanced at him. Gabriel avoided looking at her, and gave the driver the address of Penny's apartment.

"Step on it, will ya?" Gabriel added. "Before we catch pneumonia."

The driver grumbled, but threw the cab into gear and sped off through the murky streets. Penny said nothing as they rode, the cab's windshield wipers beating a steady rhythm against the front glass. Gabriel glanced at her. She sat back as far as she could in the seat, staring ahead of her with a slight furrow in her pretty brow, her arms folded tightly.

A gentleman would scoot close to her and wrap her up in his arms to keep her warm.

Gabriel stayed where he was.

"You missed your date with Vivian tonight," Penny murmured.

Gabriel took a breath and folded his own arms.

"Yeah, I guess I did," he muttered. "I'll call her later." Penny didn't answer, nor did she look at him.

Finally, they pulled up in front of Penny's narrow brick apartment building—one of those ladies' boarding houses where men were only allowed into the entryway and the tiny front parlor. Thankfully, Harry and his goons had just taken Gabriel's gun and knife, but not his wallet or badge, so Gabriel was able to pass the driver the correct fare—even if it was soggy.

"Hang around for a second, I'll be right back," Gabriel told him, then opened the door and got out, helping Penny out, too. They dashed through the rain, up the stairs, and Penny pressed the buzzer. In a few moments, Mrs. Rollings, the landlady, came to the door.

"Good heavens!" the white-haired, portly lady cried as she opened the door and pulled Penny inside. "Miss Creek, Mr. Kelley, what's happened to the two of you?"

"We had a little adventure, but it's nothing, Mrs. Rollings," Penny laughed as the two spilled into the warm, dry entryway. Gabriel glanced around. It was a modest establishment, but Mrs.

Rollings—who was originally from Kansas—kept a clean, cozy and well-lit boarding house.

"Let me get you a towel, dear!" Mrs. Rollings declared, and dashed off through a side door. "I'd better get going before the cab drives off," Gabriel said quietly, running his hand through his dripping hair again. Penny watched him carefully.

"What about Harry?"

"What about him?" Gabriel asked.

"He wanted you to lay off, didn't he?" Gabriel heaved a sigh.

"Yeah, he did."

"And?" she pressed.

Gabriel looked at her.

"Maybe just let me worry about that, okay Penny?"

Penny said nothing, her eyebrows drawing together delicately. Gabriel smiled crookedly. "Don't worry about me, Pen," he said—and before he knew it, he had lifted his hand and touched her chin.

In that moment, he realized it would be the most natural thing in the world for him just to lean in and give her a kiss.

He dropped his hand.

"I'll see you tomorrow," he said, backing toward the door.

"Yes, Mr. Kelley," she murmured, wrapping her arms around herself again. He took hold of the doorknob, then looked at her again.

"Take a cab this time, not the L," he said seriously. "And come in the front door, not that side door."

She smiled faintly.

"Yes, Mr. Kelley."

He returned the smile, and pulled the door open just as Mrs. Rollings reappeared with the towel for Penny. Without looking back again, Gabriel dove back out into the rain and jumped into the cab. He gave him his own address, and sank back into the seat...

Only now glancing back at Penny's windows.

She'd never know how his heart had plunged through the floor when he'd realized Harry had taken her.

She'd never know what he'd felt when she had disappeared under that black water.

She'd never know. She couldn't.

He shifted and reached up to his jacket—making sure his badge still lay securely within his inside pocket.

Don't miss out!

Visit the website below and you can sign up to receive emails whenever Alydia Rackham publishes a new book. There's no charge and no obligation.

https://books2read.com/r/B-A-MQLEB-AOWBD

Did you love *Gabriel Kelley: Chicago Detective*? Then you should read *The Ignominious Mister Tipp*[1] by Alydia Rackham!

An unlikely duo and an ice-cold murder case... Lucinda Holliday--an educated lady with fiery red hair and an aloof disposition--must bargain help from the striking-but-volatile American, Mr. Tipp: a disgraced detective turned opium addict...For he is the only man on earth who can possibly solve the mystery of her father's senseless murder.*Plunge into the romance and danger of 1870's London as this incompatible pair tangle with the cold case that destroyed both their lives, all while being haunted and hunted by the most elusive and insidious murderer in the world.*

Read more at https://alydiarackham642036291.wordpress.com/.

---

1. https://books2read.com/u/4jY9qD

2. https://books2read.com/u/4jY9qD

Also by Alydia Rackham

Alydia Rackham's Retellings
Bauldr's Tears: Retelling Loki's Fate
Ghost: Retelling the Phantom of the Opera
The Tailor of Semenov: Retelling the Legend of Anastasia
Christmas Parcel: Sequel to Charles Dickens' Classic "A Christmas Carol"

Lady Rackham
Lady Rackham: An Unusual Tale of Piracy Upon the High Seas
Blackbeard's Sword: The Continuing Adventures of Captain Lady Rackham

Stardust
Stardust

The Curse-Breaker Series
Scales: A Fresh Telling of Beauty and the Beast
Glass: Retelling the Snow Queen

Tide: Retelling the Little Mermaid
Curse-Maker: The Tale of Gwiddon Crow

The Legacy of Constantin

The Last Constantin: A Novel of the Original Vampire

The Pendywick Place

The Mute of Pendywick Place and the Torn Page
The Mute of Pendywick Place and the Scarlet Gown
The Mute of Pendywick Place and the River Thames
The Mute of Pendywick Place and the Irish Gamble
The Mute of Pendywick Place and the Ghost of Robin Hood's Bay
The Mute of Anthony College and the Three Professors
Dear David: Being the Private Diary of Basil Atticus Collingwood
The Ignominious Mister Tipp

The Tailor of Semenov

The Tailor of Semenov - Part 1
The Tailor of Semenov - Part Two
The Tailor of Semenov - Part 3
The Tailor of Semenov - Part 4

Standalone

The Last Scene
Knight of Novus: A Post-Dystopia Novel
Bureau of Investigative Time-Travel: Episodes 1-8

Gabriel Kelley: Chicago Detective
Amatus
Linnet and the Prince
The Oxford Street Coffee House Detectives and the Case of the Young
Patrician Lady
The Web of Tenebrae: The Chronicle of KL-62

Watch for more at https://alydiarackham642036291.wordpress.com/.

About the Author

Alydia Rackham is a daughter of Jesus Christ. She has written more than thirty original novels of many genres, including fantasy, time-travel, steampunk, modern romance, historical fiction, science fiction, and allegory. She is also a singer, actress, avid traveler, artist, and animal lover.
Read more at https://alydiarackham642036291.wordpress.com/.